Lovingly dedicated to the ancestors who guide me;
Mom, Monty, Dad, and Nina who love and encourage me;
and all of those individuals who need to know that their
story is worth telling.

www.mascotbooks.com

Carefree, Like Me!: Chapter 1: Root the Brave

For more information, please contact:
Mascot Books
560 Herndon Parkway #120
Herndon, VA 20170
info@mascotbooks.com

Library of Congress Control Number: 2016919539

CPSIA Code: PRT0117A
ISBN-13: 978-1-68401-098-1

Printed in the United States

Carefree, Like Me!

~Chapter 1: Root the Brave~

by Rashad Malik Davis

Amir and Neena were best friends
who did everything together!
Hopscotch, leapfrog, hide and seek—
you name it. They did whatever.

But as all good things tend to go,
Their fun eventually came to a slow.

They grew bored of all their games,
Yet still had a need for adventure they could not tame.

So, crying and annoyed, Amir came home and exclaimed, "There's nothing left to do! We're tired of all our games!"

With a laugh and a hug, Dad wiped away the tears,
Chased away the doubts, and soothed the fears.

"If you open your eyes," Dad said as his eyes shined,
"You won't believe the treasures you'll find."

"There's one place you haven't explored! A place too large to fit.
It's where heroes roam free, and it's called the land of the spirit."
Amir looked up in wonder and delight.
He jumped and yelled, "How do I go? When's the next flight?"

Dad reached into a nearby chest with a grin,
And pulled a shiny necklace from deep within.
"You're ready for an adventure you won't want to miss.
You just need a loving heart, an open mind, and this..."

He gently placed the mysterious item 'round Amir's neck.
But even with Dad's love, Amir still felt like a wreck.

Outside, Neena yelled for her friend, wanting to split,
But when she saw his new necklace, she just stared at it.
In the spirit of good fun, and to be a tease,
She snatched it from him and ran away fast as the breeze.

Shocked and angry, Amir gave chase,
But then Neena slipped and fell flat on her face.
Hitting the ground, she let the necklace go,
That's when they noticed it'd started to glow!

Before they could run,
the necklace sucked them through space and time,
And they landed in a new world on their backside!

The place where they landed was bright and rainbow lit.
Beams of light danced so wild their eyes had to squint.
Amir smiled and said, "I think we're in the land of the spirit!"
But Neena said, "You must be crazy. I don't believe that one bit!"

From out of nowhere a funny little creature appeared.
Its eyes shone like diamonds and it grinned ear to ear.
Upon spotting the two, it jumped, danced, and sang with glee,
"Our heroes have come! Our realm can finally be free!"

Confused, Neena cried, "What are you talking about,
you odd little thing?
Where are we? What's with that song that you sing?"
But it happily replied, "A world out of balance!
A mighty plea!
The necklace chose two halves of a whole, can't you see?"

"The heroes may leave once the deed is done,
Until then neither may leave, not even a one!"
It giggled and snorted as above them it soared,
Then it zoomed off and disappeared behind a solid red door.

The confused best friends ran through the door,
But what they saw on the other side made their jaws hit the floor.
They were in a gigantic palace of some kind,
So splendid and lovely it nearly made them blind.

But to their surprise the kingdom was bare.
A silent, spooky quiet hung heavy in the air.
From behind a stone block a small creature quivered.
Amir stepped forward to talk, but it just whimpered and shivered.

"What's the matter my friend? Why are you so scared?"
"The monsters under King Root's bed!
He told us to hide so we'd be spared!"

"He hasn't left his chambers for days, weeks, and months,
But since you two don't seem afraid, maybe you've got the right stuff!"
The creature poked and pushed 'til they got to the chamber gates,
Then it quickly ran off and left them to their fates.

The king was massive and strong, but he sat shaking on his bed.
He was scared and filled with the deepest dread.
"That scratching beneath! Please tell me you hear,
I just know monsters are drawing ever near!
Please take a look underneath, I swear it'll be quick.
All I know is that I just can't do it."

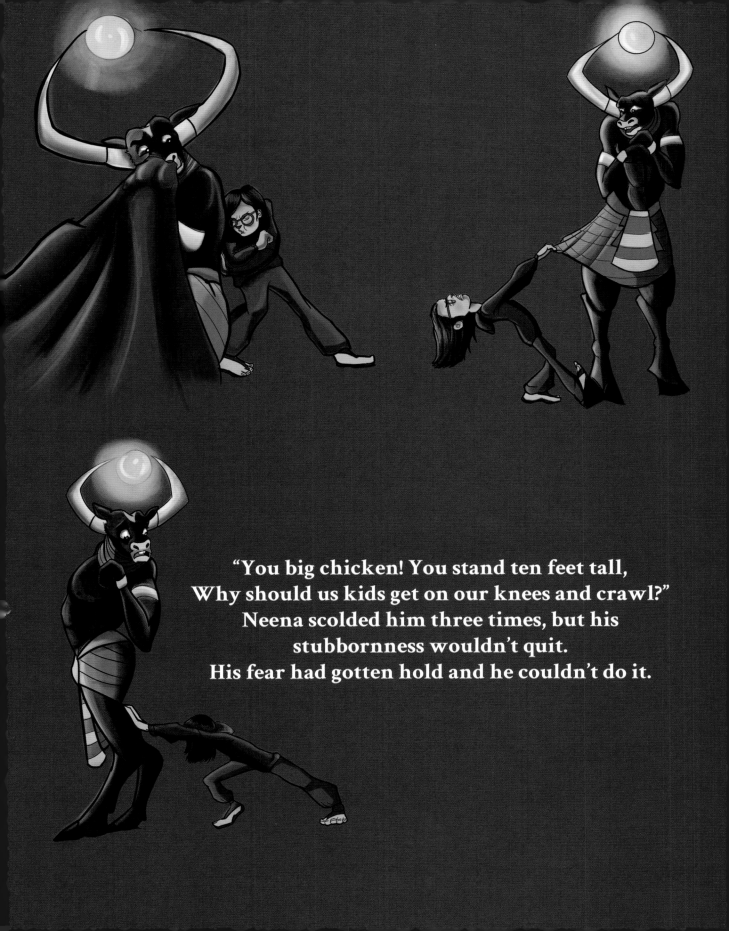

"You big chicken! You stand ten feet tall,
Why should us kids get on our knees and crawl?"
Neena scolded him three times, but his
stubbornness wouldn't quit.
His fear had gotten hold and he couldn't do it.

Just then, Amir had a thought:
A perfect lesson that his Dad had taught.
"I've been afraid many a time,
But Dad says it's not about the fall, but how you try again and climb.
Meet your fears head on and don't back down.
Surely that will return your brave, royal crown!"

Amir smiled and finally Root agreed.
It seemed all he needed was a little sympathy.
Neena took his hand, and all three bravely looked for the beast,
Imagining a monster of fur, claws, and sharp teeth.

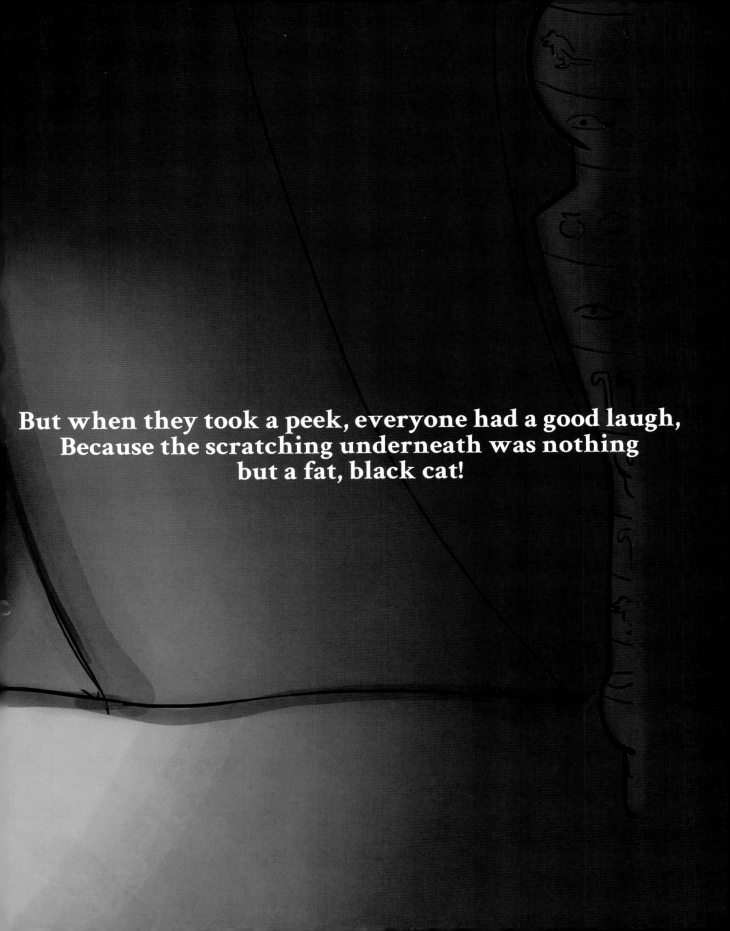

But when they took a peek, everyone had a good laugh,
Because the scratching underneath was nothing
but a fat, black cat!

King Root hugged them tight and roared with delight.
Finally the dark had lifted off this long night.
He burst from his chambers in kingly power,
And his kingdom cheered loudly enough to reach the highest tower.

Before they could celebrate and before they could revel,
The necklace shone red and pulled them from the temple.
Root waved goodbye and so did they
As the necklace sucked them far away.

Amir and Neena landed with a bump to their heads,
And saw that one part of the necklace now shone red.
The new world they were in was orange and blue,
As they traded looks and said, "Well, now what do we do...?"

List of Carefree, Like Me! Backers

Alan	Cyrus	Jennifer	Mark	Rubab
Alex M.	Danielle	Jinhyun	Marquel	Rucha
Alex O.	Dave D.	Joan	Mateo	Ryan
Alex W.	David G.	Johnny	Matt	Sam
Alexi	Devon	Joke	Matthew J.	Samantha P.
Alexis	Devyn	Katherine C.	Matthew K.	Sandhya
Allison K.	Eleanor	Katherine W.	Mahias	Sarah
Allyson	Elizabeth	Katie D.	Maureen	Sebastian
Ama	Emani	Katie R.	Michael H.	Sheryl
Ami	Emily	Kelvin	Michael O.	Shirley
Ann	Erica	Kemec	Mike C.	Sof Rac
Anthony	Erick	Khadijah	Myhana	Sonya
Anya	Frank B.	Kim P.	Natalie	Stephanie Q.
Ariel	Frank F.	Kimberly S.	Natalie P.	Stephanie V.
Arielle	Fred	Kit	Nina	Susan
Babisa	Gabrielle	Krylataja	Nirvanna	Suyu
Bethany	Genesis	Laura	Noam	Talia
Boreta	Grainne	Lawrence Bo.	Olamide	Tammy
Bruce	Groom	Lawrence Br.	Olive & Michael	Taurean
Candace	Hailey	Lexi	Owen	Tibby
Cara	Hana	Lisa	Peter	Tory & Curtis
Casseia	Ikenna	Lori-Ann	Raymond	Uju
Cassie	Indigo	Louis	Rhey	Vinay
Catherine	Isaiah	Lura	Rodney	Will
Cathy C.	Jade	Luriel	Rohit	Will E.
Chris	Jasmine	Maalika	Rose	Zak & Leah
Cory	Jasond	Maggie	Rosemary	

About the Author

Author/illustrator Rashad Malik Davis can most often be found sketching, writing, or engaging in excited dialogue about the magic and beauty—both seen and unseen—of our diverse world. Though this is his first picture book written and illustrated on his own, he has illustrated for a #1 bestselling children's book on Amazon entitled *Sunne's Gift: How Sunne Overcame Bullying to Reclaim God's Gift*. Rashad resides in New Jersey with family and a wide array of pencils, pens, and unfinished how-to books. For more or to follow his work, please visit his website at www.ramalikillustrations.com.